Super Special #2

The Case of
the
Million-Dollar Mystery

Read all the Jigsaw Jones Mysteries

And Don't Miss

Coming Soon

Super Special #2

The Case of
the
Million-Dollar Mystery

by James Preller
illustrated by Jamie Smith
cover illustration by R. W. Alley

A
LITTLE APPLE
PAPERBACK

SCHOLASTIC INC.
New York Toronto London Auckland Sydney
Mexico City New Delhi Hong Kong Buenos Aires

For all the great young writers (and enthusiastic readers!)
at Glenmont Elementary School.

—J.P.

ISBN 0-439-42629-4

12   5 6 7/0

Printed in the U.S.A.   40
First printing, November 2002

CONTENTS

Chapter One

Joey Eats Over

Joey Pignattano blinked nervously. The game was up, and he knew it. I took a deep breath and said, "I accuse Colonel Mustard . . . in the study . . . with the lead pipe."

Joey searched hopelessly through his playing cards. Finally, he tossed the pile onto the game board. "You win again, Jigsaw," he said with a sigh. "That's two in a row."

"Three," I murmured. "But who's counting?"

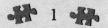

My mother knocked and came into the bedroom. "Would Joey like to stay for dinner?" she asked.

Joey was thrilled. After all, it involved his favorite activity — eating. We stuffed the Clue game board under my bed, washed our hands, and raced into the kitchen.

Inviting Joey to dinner was like asking Nolan Ryan over for a game of catch. When

it came to eating, Joey was a Hall of Famer. He'd gobble down *anything* — even food I wouldn't touch with a ten-foot hockey stick. Take broccoli, for example.

In fact, take it far away. Let's face it: Broccoli looks funny, it smells funny, and it tastes funny — but no one's laughing. Except for my mom, who acts like broccoli is the greatest invention since Velcro.

"I *love* broccoli," Joey proudly announced from his seat at the corner of the table. "It's yummy in my tummy."

I nearly spewed my milk. "Hey, you can't trust Joey's opinion," I advised my parents. "He once ate a worm for a dollar."

My father stopped cutting into his chicken breast. "You ate a worm?" he repeated.

"It wasn't so bad, Mr. Jones," Joey answered cheerfully. "Three chews and a swallow. I'd do it again for a quarter," he offered.

"No, please!" my mom quickly stated. "That won't be necessary."

"What did the worm taste like?" asked my brother Daniel.

Joey gave it some thought. "Like chicken," he concluded.

Hillary dropped a drumstick and pushed her plate away. "*Blech!* That's it, I'm sooo tired of living with boys! Mom, may I please be excused?"

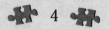 4

"You'll stay here and finish your dinner," my mother answered. Then she turned to me. "You, too, Theodore. No dessert until you eat everything on your plate."

A few minutes later, when no one was looking, I made my move. *Plop, plop, plop* — I dropped the last three pieces of broccoli into my glass of milk. They sank to the bottom, hidden in the milky whiteness. "All done," I announced, showing my empty plate. "What's for dessert?"

Chapter Two
Green Milk

"Finish your milk first," my dad said.

I held my stomach and made a face. "It doesn't taste right," I said. "I think the milk went sour."

Joey instantly downed his glass with a happy *slurp*. Under a thick white mustache, he crowed, "Tastes great to me, Jigsaw!"

I shot him the evil eye.

"Go ahead, drink up," my dad insisted.

Here I was again, up that same old river. Without a paddle.

I tried changing the subject. "We're

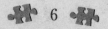 6

learning about inventions in school," I said. "Isn't that right, Joey?"

Joey nodded happily. "Ms. Gleason just read us a really funny book called *Ben and Me* by Robert Lawson. It's about this nutty mouse who lives with Benjamin Franklin. And I just got a library book about Thomas Alva Edison. It's called, um, *Thomas Alva Edison*."

"Gee, what a catchy title," Hillary murmured.

Joey continued, "Edison became a millionaire because he invented practically everything. He had a famous saying . . . um . . ." Joey paused, trying to remember the exact words. "Oh, yeah, it was something like, 'Science is one hundred percent perspiration'!"

My father chuckled. "Not exactly, Joey. Edison said, 'Genius is one percent inspiration and ninety-nine percent perspiration.'"

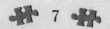

I began to sweat, too. Because my milk was slowly turning green! I leaned forward on my elbow, hoping to hide the glass from view. "Ms. Gleason wants us to come up with our own ideas for inventions," I said.

Joey accidentally knocked against the table leg for about the twelfth time, nearly spilling my milk. "Careful, Joey!" I complained.

"It's not Joey's fault," Daniel pointed out. "He can't pull in his chair. The dumb table leg keeps getting in the way."

"The table is *not* dumb," my mother said. "And you know we don't use that word in this house."

"Table?" Joey wondered.

"No, the D-word," my mom said. "But I am sorry if you're uncomfortable, Joey. It is a little crowded."

"I'm okay," Joey replied. "Maybe a cookie would help me feel better."

My father cleared his throat. "Before we

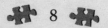 8

start handing out cookies, I'd still like to see Jigsaw finish his milk."

"But Dad!" I protested.

My stomach flopped when I saw the sly grin on my father's face. Come to think of it, I wasn't crazy about the twinkle in his eye, either. I glanced at my milk. By now, it had turned a sickly shade of green. Little green flecks had floated to the top.

"Hey, what happened to your milk?" Joey asked.

My dad shook his head and laughed. "Oh, Jigsaw. Won't you ever learn? We've seen all these tricks before. Remember the golden rule: You can't hide broccoli in a glass of milk."

Then he told me to drink it.

"If I barf, you'll be sorry," I warned.

"Bottoms up," he replied cheerfully.

Chapter Three

A Surprise Visitor

Suddenly, my dog, Rags, started barking at the front door. It didn't matter how many times people came to our house. For Rags, it was *always* The Biggest Surprise on Earth. Rags ran around in circles. Three seconds later — *dingdong* — the doorbell rang.

"I'll get it!" I cried.

Nicole Rodriguez stood at the front door. She seemed uneasy.

"Don't worry about Rags," I told her. "He gets excited whenever someone comes to the door. Go figure."

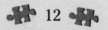

"I've got a dog at home," Nicole answered. "Her name is Zippy. I love dogs." Nicole smiled at Rags and bent down to pet him.

Slurp! Rags gave Nicole a wet, sloppy kiss. After wiping her mouth, Nicole spoke hurriedly. Her hands fluttered like sparrows. "I'm so glad you're home, Jigsaw. Ever since I found this horrible note I've been —" Nicole abruptly stopped talking. Her gaze fixed on a spot above my right shoulder. "Oh, hi, Joey," she said in a gloomy voice. "I didn't know you were here."

Nicole took a small step backward, like she suddenly didn't want to be here anymore.

"What's wrong?" I asked.

Nicole swallowed hard. She looked at Joey, then me, then back to Joey again. And I finally understood. "Sorry, Joey," I said. "Nicole is here on business. I'd better speak with her in private."

"That's okay, Jigsaw," Joey replied. "I've got to get home anyway. I'm working on a very important experiment."

"For school?" I wondered.

Joey shrugged. "It's sort of a surprise. But I'll give you a hint." Joey cupped his hand around his mouth and whispered: "I'm hatching eggs."

"Eggs?" I echoed.

"Shhh," Joey replied solemnly, putting a finger to his lips.

I nodded, not knowing exactly why. The three of us went into the kitchen. Joey thanked my parents, hungrily shoved a few cookies into his pockets, and headed out the door.

"Let me call Mila," I said to Nicole.

"Do you have to?" Nicole asked. "I was hoping we could keep this between us."

"Mila is my partner," I answered. "We always work together."

"Yes, but . . ."

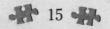

"You can trust us," I said.

Nicole pulled the hair away from her face. She nodded once. Five minutes later, I was seated at my desk in the basement. Across from me sat Nicole and Mila. Behind my back hung a sign: **JIGSAW JONES, PRIVATE EYE.** It was nothing fancy. Just a hunk of wood with my name on it. But it did the job.

Just like me.

Nicole unfolded a piece of blue construction paper. "I found this in school this morning," she explained.

It was a short note. Just five words. A total of fourteen letters. Still, it gave me goose bumps.

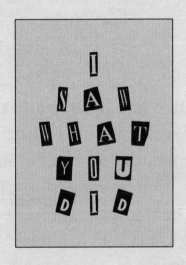

Chapter Four
The Note

Each letter had been neatly cut out and glued down. The paper that the letters were printed on was slick and crisp — probably from a magazine. The letters definitely didn't come from a newspaper.

"Creepy," Mila said in a hush. "Where did you find this?"

"It was stuffed in my desk. I found it there after recess," Nicole explained.

"Did you find anything else?" I asked.

Nicole shook her head. "No, nothing. Just the note."

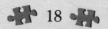

I exchanged glances with Mila. In a soft voice, Mila explained to Nicole that this might be a case of blackmail.

"Blackmail?" Nicole repeated.

"Yes," Mila said. "It's when somebody knows something bad about you that you don't want anyone else to know. For the right price, the blackmailer will keep quiet."

Nicole struggled to understand. "So you're telling me . . . if I give this person money, they won't tell anyone what they saw me do?"

"Yes and no," I answered. "First of all, the blackmailer — *if* he or she is a blackmailer — has not asked for anything yet. So in this case, the note reads more like a warning."

"A warning? A warning about what?!"

I shrugged. "I guess whatever it is that you did, well, maybe you shouldn't do it anymore."

Nicole chirped, "But I don't *know* what I did!"

"Think," Mila urged. "Is there *anything* at all? Did you hurt someone's feelings? Did you take something you shouldn't have? Is there any reason why someone might be unhappy with you?"

Nicole shook her head, her eyes fixed on a faraway place. "Maybe there is something. . . ." Nicole began doubtfully. "Oh, I don't know. *Everybody* does something wrong. Nobody is a perfect angel all the time. How come I'm the only one who gets a creepy note?!"

I went upstairs to get Nicole a glass of grape juice. Returning to my desk, I explained, "For a dollar a day, we make problems go away. Mila and I can check this out for you. We'll ask around. We'll track down clues. Maybe we'll bump into some answers along the way."

Nicole handed me a crisp dollar bill.

Good old George Washington. He had a lousy haircut, but I always liked seeing his face. "That should do it for now," I said. "We'll see you in school tomorrow."

Mila placed a hand on Nicole's shoulder. "I'll walk you home, Nicole. Just try to relax. We'll get to the bottom of this."

Nicole nodded. "And in the meantime," she chirped, "I'll be extra, extra good."

Chapter Five

Top Secret

On Tuesday morning, I caught up with Joey on the way to room 201. "How's the great egg experiment going?" I asked.

"Not so great," he glumly answered. "I keep breaking the eggs."

"Oh?"

"I think the nest is wrong," Joey confided. "It needs more cushions and stuff."

While I was scratching my head over that one, Ralphie Jordan sidled up beside me. "I need a detective," he whispered. "But let's talk later, when no else is around."

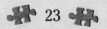 23

"Sure," I said. Hmmm. Looked like it was going to be a busy week for Jigsaw Jones, Private Eye.

In class, Ms. Gleason talked to us about inventions. Everybody was pretty excited.

"All inventions start with an idea," Ms. Gleason told us. "Inventions can be anything — the Frisbee, chocolate chip cookies, a Band-Aid, a zipper, even seat belts for dogs. When you think about it, our world is full of inventions. And many of them are very simple. Many things that we take for granted today didn't exist until an inventor dreamed them up."

"Sure, that's easy . . . if you're a major brain," complained Helen Zuckerman.

"I disagree," Ms. Gleason replied. "You don't have to be a genius to come up with a new idea. An inventor only needs three things:

CURIOSITY
IMAGINATION
HARD WORK

"In fact, Helen, many children have created new inventions. A teenage boy in Maine came up with the idea for earmuffs. An eleven-year-old invented the Popsicle."

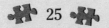

Eddie Becker raised his hand. He waved it around, moaning and groaning, "Ooh, oooh, ooooh."

"Eddie, do you have a question?" she asked.

It was like asking a shark if it had teeth.

"An inventor can get really rich, right, Ms. Gleason?" Eddie asked. Mila caught my eye and smiled. Typical Eddie. Becoming rich was his one big goal in life.

Ms. Gleason nodded. "Yes, Eddie. If the invention becomes very popular, the inventor is bound to make lots of money."

Eddie smiled broadly. "That's good. Because last night I came up with a million-dollar idea."

"Really?" Ms. Gleason commented. "Please tell us all about it."

Eddie shook his head. "I'll show *you*, Ms. Gleason. But I don't want anyone else to know about it."

"Come on, Eddie!" Bobby Solofsky shouted. "Tell us what it is!"

"Yeah, Eddie," barked Bigs Maloney.

"No way," Eddie shot back. "This idea is going to turn me into a millionaire. It's top secret until I say so." At this, Eddie leaned back in his chair, crossed his arms, and clutched a large envelope close to his chest.

I noticed the bright red letters on the envelope. It read TOP SECRET.

But it wouldn't be for long.

Chapter Six

Ralphie's Problem

I scribbled a picture of a mad scientist. He was mixing secret potions. Next to him, I drew a picture of Mila. Above her head I wrote, **HIS FAITHFUL HELPER, IGOR.**

When I showed it to Mila, she rolled her eyes and made a noise like this: *Harrrumff.* Go figure.

What's "harrrumff" mean, anyway? Maybe it's Swedish for "You made my nose too big."

During DEAR time — that's Drop Everything And Read time — Eddie placed his "top secret" envelope on Ms. Gleason's desk. "This is for your eyes only, Ms. Gleason," Eddie stated. "You promise, right?"

"For my eyes only," Ms. Gleason repeated. "I'll take a look at it later tonight."

A few minutes later, we had snack recess. Then Ms. Gleason let us outside. A door in our classroom opened to the playground. We swarmed out the door like bees from a honey tree. Mila and I stood by the tire swing, talking things over. Actually, she sat. I pushed.

"Did Nicole have anything more to say last night?" I asked.

Mila shook her head. "Not exactly. But I feel like she's not telling us everything."

I agreed. "If we only knew *what* she did, it might help us find out who left the note. Right now, everyone in room 201 is a suspect."

"Except for me and you," Mila pointed out.

"Nicole acted weird when she saw Joey," I told her. "Maybe Nicole suspects Joey."

Mila thought for a moment. "She probably didn't want anyone else to know about the note," she suggested.

I shrugged. "Could be."

While spinning in circles, Mila said, "Look, here comes Ralphie."

"Hi, guys." Ralphie glanced from side to side, making sure no one was around. In a hushed voice, he said, "I found this note in my backpack last night."

He showed us the note:

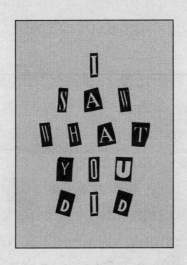

It was exactly like the one Nicole had shown us the night before. The same words, the same cutout letters from a magazine.

Only this time, the construction paper was green, not blue.

"It looks like our blackmailer has been busy," I commented.

"Huh?"

"You aren't the only one who got a note like this," Mila told Ralphie.

This seemed to cheer him up. "Really? That's good. I mean, it's not so lonely, I guess. Do you guys think you can solve the mystery?"

"Does Britney Spears have a belly button?" I replied.

"Uh, yeah."

"There's your answer," I said. "Do you have any idea when someone could have slipped this note into your backpack?"

Ralphie shook his head. "It just hangs in my cubby all day," he said. "It's always in plain sight."

"Except during recess . . . or gym

class . . . or lunch," Mila noted to Ralphie and me.

"I guess there's one less name on our list of suspects," I told Mila.

"But we don't *have* a list of suspects," she observed.

Mila had a point. I went back into the classroom to get my detective journal. During snack recess, kids walked in and out of room 201 whenever they wanted. Sometimes to get something, like a hat and gloves. Sometimes just to go to the bathroom. I ran into Bobby Solofsky on my way inside. That is, he bumped into me.

"Watch it, Solofsky," I complained.

Bobby grinned. "Oh, sorry, Jigsaw. I was looking under there."

"Under where?"

Solofsky laughed like a hyena. Pointing and giggling, he chanted, "You said *underwear*! You said *underwear*!"

"Very clever," I muttered over my shoulder. "That's the oldest joke in the book."

I searched in my desk for my journal and promised myself that I'd clean it out one of these days.

Ah-choo.

Someone sneezed.

I wasn't alone.

There was someone hiding behind Ms. Gleason's desk.

Chapter Seven

The Suspects

I rose silently from my chair.

Slowly, I inched toward Ms. Gleason's desk. I heard papers rustling and a voice mumbling, "Oh, heavens to Betsy."

I peered around the corner of the desk. There was a man kneeling on the ground, fumbling with something under the desk. I noted tasseled black loafers. Argyle socks. Brown slacks. It could only be one person.

"Principal Rogers!" I exclaimed.

BONK!

I guess I startled him. Because at the

sound of my voice — *whap*! Mr. Rogers quickly sat up, bashing his head against the underside of Ms. Gleason's desk.

Principal Rogers stood up, wincing. "Oh, hello, Jigsaw," he said. In his arms he carried a messy stack of books, folders, and assorted papers. He blinked painfully.

"Did I scare you?"

Mr. Rogers carefully placed the leaning stack in several piles on Ms. Gleason's desk. He rubbed his head. "It's been one of those days," he said. "Mrs. Garcia is out sick today. So I'm running around like a chicken with its head cut off. Is Ms. Gleason outside?" he wondered.

I nodded. "Yes."

"Right, right," Mr. Rogers replied. He suddenly seemed to be in a big hurry. "Please tell her that I dropped off the folders and picked up her notes for the meeting."

I scooped up the stacks of papers and

piled them into his arms. Mr. Rogers wobbled out the door, tottering awkwardly.

That left me alone in the room. I glanced at Ms. Gleason's desk. There was a glass jar filled with hard candy. The peppermint looked nice. And the butterscotch called to me in a little voice, "Eat me, eat me."

I lifted the lid and grabbed a candy. No one would ever know.

Or so I thought.

Outside once again, Mila and I wrote out a list of suspects. It included everyone in room 201, except for Ms. Gleason. We left out Ralphie and Nicole's names, too. We doubted they sent notes to themselves.

SUSPECTS

Bigs Maloney	Danika Starling
Mike Radcliff	Joey Pignattano
Lucy Hiller	Kim Lewis
Helen Zuckerman	Eddie Becker
Athena Lorenzo	Bobby Solofsky
Stringbean Noonan	

I circled Solofsky's name. "He's always trouble."

Mila nodded in agreement.

"Helen is another prime suspect," Mila added. "You remember all those pranks she used to pull."

I remembered. Who could forget the time she put Jell-O in Athena's gym sneakers?

"What about Bigs?" I asked.

Mila squinched her face. "Not his style."

"Probably right. He'd put someone in a headlock before he wrote a note," I observed. "Still, we've got to talk to everyone on this list."

"Hey, we forgot Geetha!" Mila exclaimed, slapping her forehead.

I laughed. "Geetha's so quiet, I forget she's there sometimes."

I added the name Geetha Nair to the list. Then I asked Mila, "Do you think we should try to find out what kinds of things people have done wrong?"

"What do you mean?" she asked.

"The way I figure it," I replied, "this blackmailer has been watching people. If they do something bad, they get a note."

"But why isn't there a ransom?" Mila pondered. "Someone could make a lot of money off this scam. But our blackmailer doesn't seem to want *anything*."

I lifted my hat and scratched my head. "Everybody wants *something*," I mumbled. "We just have to figure out what."

Chapter Eight

The Million-Dollar Robbery

Eddie noticed it immediately. "Ms. Gleason," he asked, "did you hide my million-dollar idea?"

Ms. Gleason glanced at her desk. "Why, no, Eddie. I never touched it."

"Don't kid around, Ms. Gleason," Eddie said. "That invention could make me rich."

Ms. Gleason leafed through the papers on her desk. She leaned over and checked the floor. "That's strange," she said.

Eddie leaped out of his chair and searched through Ms. Gleason's garbage can. He demanded that everyone look in their desks. Eddie pulled his hair, fumed, and howled. Other than that, I'd say he took it pretty well.

"Eddie, please calm down," Ms. Gleason said in soothing tones. "I'm sure it will turn up somewhere."

"Who stole it?!" Eddie shouted. He turned and pointed at each one of us. "Someone in this room is a thief — and I'm gonna find out who!"

"That's enough, Eddie," Ms. Gleason ordered. Her voice was stern. "Sit down and be quiet. I won't have that kind of talk in this classroom. Do you understand?"

Eddie scowled, then nodded. He understood. But he wasn't happy about it.

A few moments later, I slipped him my business card.

NEED A MYSTERY SOLVED?
Call Jigsaw Jones
or Mila Yeh!
for a dollar a day,
we make problems go away.

CALL 555-4523 or 555-4374

"You're hired," he whispered. Then he turned his back to me, still fuming.

I wrote in my journal:

CLIENT: Eddie Becker
CASE: The Million-Dollar Mystery

I exchanged glances with Mila, rubbing a finger across my nose. It was our secret signal. We were on the case. I thought about the mystery. Maybe our blackmailer had switched to robbery. The envelope was on Ms. Gleason's desk, we went outside for recess, and it vanished before we returned. That gave the robber fifteen minutes, tops. Who else had been in room 201 during snack recess? We needed to ask around. Solofsky was, I knew that. And I was, too, but I was alone.

A terrible thought crossed my mind. It seemed to sink like a stone, settling in my stomach. *I wasn't alone.* Principal Rogers was there, too. He was messing around near Ms. Gleason's desk. I had startled him.

He seemed nervous and jumpy. And he was in a big hurry to leave.

The thought was unthinkable. But there I was, thinking it. Could Mr. Rogers have stolen the envelope? For a million-dollar idea, I guessed, anything was possible.

Yeesh.

The good news was I already had a suspect for the case. The bad news was . . . it was my school principal.

Chapter Nine

My Invention

Hillary stood across from me, arms crossed, foot tapping impatiently. "You've been on the phone all day," she hissed.

"I've got to hang up, Mike," I spoke into the phone. "My sister is having a cow."

I guess I couldn't blame Hillary. I had been talking on the phone for a while. I learned a lot, too. Between Mila and me, we discovered that five more kids in our class had gotten notes — Lucy, Bigs, Athena, Kim, and Mike. Each note was the same in

every way except one: The color of the construction paper changed each time.

Our list of suspects was shrinking. I wondered if the blackmailer could have sent a note to him- or herself, just to throw us off the trail. But more important than that, I still couldn't figure out the motive. Why send all those creepy notes? Why not ask for a ransom? And were the notes somehow connected to Eddie's missing envelope?

Geetha told Mila that she saw me, Bobby, Helen, and Kim all go in and out of the classroom during morning recess. Helen and Kim admitted as much, but they'd gone in together. Solofsky claimed he saw Geetha go into the classroom. Geetha denied it.

One of them was lying.

Unfortunately, I still had spelling homework and half an hour of reading to do. Plus I had to start working on my invention. Yeesh. How's a detective supposed to get any work done?

After I finished my homework, I found my dad in the basement. He was carving wooden ducks. Don't ask why. Nobody can figure it out. My brother Billy says, "Dad's a little *quackers*."

"Hey, kiddo," he greeted me.

"Hi, Dad. How's it going?"

"Just ducky," he joked. Then he eyed me closely. "What do you want, Jigsaw?"

"Me?" I said. "I don't want anything. Can't a kid come down to see how his dear old dad is doing? Would you like anything? Some grape juice or roasted nuts or something?"

"Peace and quiet would be nice . . ." he murmured.

I sighed.

He continued carving the feathers.

I sighed again, louder this time.

"Maybe there is something . . ." I finally admitted.

I told my dad how Ms. Gleason said that many inventions aren't really brand-new ideas at all. Inventors often take old ideas and make them better.

"Like what, for example?"

"Like adding ridges to potato chips," I answered.

"I see what you mean." My dad nodded. "Have you got an idea?"

I did. "You know how a detective will sometimes hold a glass up to a wall so he can hear what's going on in the other room? Well, it doesn't work so great. Besides, people notice that sort of thing."

"So you'd like to invent something more *discreet*?"

"I don't know about that," I replied. "But it would be nice if it was sneakier."

My dad raised an eyebrow. "Got any ideas?"

I told him that I had a few. But I couldn't

build it without his help. We stayed up late that night, digging through the supplies in his workshop. We screwed together a small wooden box, ripped up an old radio, and we were on our way.

The invention turned out awesome.

Of course, I didn't tell my dad that I was planning on using my new invention the very next day, when I spied on the school principal.

For some reason, I figured he'd rather not know.

Parents are funny that way.

Chapter Ten

Pig Latin

Mila and I sat together on the morning bus ride to school.

"Oodgay orningmay, igsawjay," she said.

"Huh?"

"Anyway ewsnay onway hetay asecay?" Mila said, grinning.

"Take the marbles out of your mouth," I replied. "I can't understand a word..." Then it hit me. Mila was *talking* in code. She was using a secret language called pig Latin. We liked to practice it every once in a while.

Pig Latin could be tricky at first. But once you get the knack, it's not hard. A lot of kids know a little bit of pig Latin. But if you speak it very fast, most people don't know what you're talking about.

With pig Latin, if a word begins with a vowel, you add WAY at the end. So "out" becomes "outway" and "on" becomes "onway."

But if a word begins with a consonant, you move the first letter to the end of the word and add AY. So "man" becomes "anmay" and "good" becomes "oodgay."

Mila had greeted me, "Good morning, Jigsaw." Then she'd asked, "Any news on the case?"

After a while, I wanted to switch back to plain English. Talking in a secret language wears a guy out. So I said, "et'slay peaksay ormalnay, okayway?"

Mila smiled. "Uresay!"

Sure.

A jigsaw puzzle for you!

Ask an adult to help you cut out the pieces.
Then put the puzzle together. When you are
done, stick the finished picture inside your
detective journal or on a piece of paper!

I was eager to tell Mila about my plan to catch the thief who took Eddie's million-dollar idea. But first, I wanted to check my notes. I fished into my backpack, looking for my detective journal. I found it all right. Something was tucked inside it. "Look at this!" I whispered to Mila.

It was a note on purple construction paper. It read: I SAW WHAT YOU DID.

"Someone must have sneaked it into your backpack yesterday," Mila observed.

I nodded, my jaw clenched unhappily. That did it. Now it was personal. Nobody messes with my detective journal. I was going to catch this blackmailer — if it was the last thing I did. But in the back of my mind, another thought stirred. I asked myself, *What did the blackmailer see me do?* I suddenly remembered the butterscotch I nipped from Ms. Gleason's candy jar. Could someone have seen me?

Mila poked me in the ribs. "Earth to Jigsaw," she prodded. "Are you going to tell me about your plan or not?"

"Oh, yeah, sure," I said distractedly. "I need to check out the principal's office. Mr. Rogers might have stolen Eddie's million-dollar idea."

Mila frowned. "No way, Jigsaw. He's the principal."

"I saw him at the scene of the crime," I replied. "He's just another suspect to me."

I stared out the bus window, lost in thought. Finally, I said, "If only I could find a way to get into his office."

Just then, Bobby Solofsky gave a loud snort from the back of the bus. Mila pulled on her long black hair. "You could try Bobby's method," she suggested.

"How does he do it?" I asked.

Mila answered, "*He gets into trouble.*"

Chapter Eleven
Looking for Trouble

There was one problem. I'd never been sent to the principal's office before. And no matter how badly anyone acted in room 201, Ms. Gleason always handled things herself. Then it fell on me like a ton of marshmallows — the strict new lunch monitor, Ms. Hakeem. She was always sending kids to see Mr. Rogers.

The plan was set when I joined Bigs, Ralphie, Danika, Geetha, and Mila in the cafeteria. I had my invention stuffed in my front pocket. But I felt nervous and

worried. Bigs, on the other hand, seemed angry about something.

"I don't get it," Bigs growled. "My twin brothers love watching Barney on television. But what kind of dinosaur *is* Barney, anyway? A brachiosaurus? An apatosaurus? I can't figure it out. He's not like any dinosaur I've ever seen."

Danika groaned. "Bigs, like, take it easy. Barney is an actor in a goofy purple suit. It's *sooo* not a big deal."

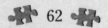

"Not a big deal?" Bigs protested. "My little brothers are growing up learning that Barney is a dinosaur. One of the coolest creatures to walk the earth. Real dinosaurs weren't like Barney. I'm telling you," he stated, "television is ruining kids today!"

"What do you want, Bigs?" Ralphie asked. "A kiddie show about an allosaurus that goes around eating everybody?"

Bigs grinned devilishly. "Yeah, I'd *love* a show like that! But seriously, Barney should at least have some horns. Even a stegosaurus had cool spikes on his tail."

Mila started humming the Barney theme song. She sang these words:

> *"Di-no-saur, with no spikes,*
> *I'm a purple dinosaur,*
> *with a great big laugh*
> *and a goofy giggle, too,*
> *why not put me in the zoo?"*

I noticed Ms. Hakeem standing nearby. "Excuse me, Ralphie," I interrupted. "But it's show time."

I reached over and grabbed a fistful of Jell-O from his tray. Now was the moment. All I had to do was throw the Jell-O and yell, "Food fight!" I hesitated, squishing the slippery Jell-O between my fingers.

Ms. Hakeem leaned forward, watching me, fearing the worst.

But I couldn't do it. Instead, I scraped off the Jell-O with a napkin.

"I've got to go," I announced.

"Go where?" Mila asked. "What are you going to do?"

"It's time for plan B," I replied.

Chapter Twelve

The Principal's Office

At our school, there was a small main office with one large desk. The school secretary, Mrs. Garcia, sat clicking at the computer keyboard. Behind her, another door led to the principal's office.

I sat down beside Mrs. Garcia. "Can I help you, Jigsaw?" she asked.

I crossed two fingers behind my back. "Um, I got into trouble. Ms. Hakeem told me to go see Mr. Rogers."

Mrs. Garcia's lips took a downward turn.

"Mr. Rogers is on the phone at the moment. But I'll see that he knows you're here."

A few moments later, Mrs. Garcia was interrupted by a call. As she listened, a smile swept across her face. "I'll deliver the message personally," she spoke into the receiver. "It will be my pleasure. And," she added, "good luck!"

Mrs. Garcia hung up. "I'll be right back," she told me. "I've got an urgent message for Coach K. It seems his wife needs a ride to the hospital." She winked. "She's going to have a baby!"

I was alone. The door to the principal's office was closed. Still, in the silence, I could hear Mr. Rogers's voice faintly through the wall.

I felt in my pocket for my invention, which I named the Listener Z-2000. Glancing back to make sure no one was watching, I set the hollow wooden box of the Listener Z-2000 on top of a bookshelf that stood against Mr. Rogers's office wall. By shifting a plant over, I hid it from sight. Then I unwound the wire and placed the plug into my ear. I returned to my seat, innocent as a fox, and listened.

Mr. Rogers's voice came through crystal clear. "Yes, I want to get rid of it quickly. You can come to see it this afternoon. But you should know, I won't sell for less than ten thousand dollars."

I feared the worst. Had Mr. Rogers stolen Eddie's invention? Was he trying to sell it? Time was running out. There was only one thing left to do.

I walked to his door and knocked three times, hard, like I meant business.

After a moment's silence, the voice on the other side of the door said, "Come in."

I took a deep breath. Grabbed the doorknob. And walked into my principal's office.

I thought he might be a thief.

But I needed proof.

Chapter Thirteen

A Close Call

Mr. Rogers spun around in his chair to face me, his eyes wide with concern.

"I'll see you at four o'clock then," he spoke into the phone. Mr. Rogers hung up the receiver. "Jigsaw, what's wrong?" he asked. "Is everything all right?"

I spoke without thinking. Somehow the words leaped from my mouth. "I think you took Eddie Becker's million-dollar invention," I said.

The minute I said it, I regretted it. Mr. Rogers stiffened. His lips tightened and his

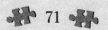

eyes narrowed. "Excuse me?" he said, not altogether kindly. "Are you suggesting that I stole —"

"Er, not exactly, um," I stammered, fumbling for words. I was used to questioning suspects, but most of them were only four feet tall. I felt very uncomfortable with Mr. Rogers staring at me. I glanced around the room for some way out of this situation. His desk was littered with papers. Behind him, on a small bookshelf, tottered stacks of folders, envelopes, and assorted papers.

I closed my eyes, remembering the time I found Mr. Rogers at Ms. Gleason's desk. Like a video, I replayed the scene in my mind, trying to see it over again. There was Mr. Rogers by the desk. He had a pile of papers in his arms. He placed several stacks on Ms. Gleason's desk. That's it — I suddenly understood! One of the stacks went on top of an envelope — Eddie's envelope. Mr. Rogers was in such a rush, he scooped up the envelope by accident! He wasn't a thief after all.

"Jigsaw?" Mr. Rogers prodded. "I asked you a question. Are you accusing me of stealing a student's work?"

"Stealing?!" I repeated. "Are you kidding? No way, Mr. Rogers. I said you took Eddie's invention . . . *by accident*."

I explained everything. "To be honest," I concluded, "I think maybe I accidentally

scooped it up and gave it to you when I piled the stacks in your arms."

Mr. Rogers smiled. "Well, yes, that could be. Let's have a look."

We found the envelope labeled TOP SECRET beneath a pile of folders. "Oh, heavens to Betsy, what a foul-up. When Mrs. Garcia isn't here, I can't keep anything straight," Mr. Rogers murmured. He handed the envelope to me. "Could you take this to Eddie? And please apologize for me."

Yeesh. That had been a close call. I jumped to the wrong conclusion — and nearly got into big trouble. But I still had one question. "Mr. Rogers, sir?"

"Yes?"

"I heard you on the phone," I admitted. "It sounded like you were selling something."

"You heard me . . . through a closed door?" he asked.

I shrugged. "Good ears, I guess."

"Yes, *I guess so*," he replied suspiciously. "Well, since you asked, I'm selling my car."

"Oh."

"And now," he said, "I have work to do, detective. That is, if you've finished questioning me."

I got out of there in a hurry, holding Eddie's envelope in my hands.

One case solved. One to go.

Chapter Fourteen

More Inventions

Back in room 201, Eddie was ecstatic to get his million-dollar idea back. Ms. Gleason, however, looked at me curiously. She asked, "Jigsaw, how did you know to go to the principal's office?"

"Just a lucky break," I answered.

Later that afternoon, Bigs Maloney showed the class his invention. "It's a nighttime-in-the-rain-puddle-stomper thingy," he told us. "See, I tied a flashlight to an ordinary umbrella. Now I can walk around in the rain at night and find puddles to stomp in."

Ms. Gleason seemed to think this was, in her word, "brilliant."

Go figure.

Mike Radcliff showed us his drawing for a motorized, revolving spaghetti fork. "A real time-saver," he claimed. "Easy on the wrists, too."

Helen Zuckerman invented a nosemuff. "It's like an earmuff," she explained, "except for noses."

Ms. Gleason glanced at the wall clock. "We have time for one more today. We'll have to finish up tomorrow."

Joey's hand shot up. "My first experiment didn't go so well," he admitted to the class. "I read in a book that as a boy Thomas Alva Edison once tried to hatch eggs by sitting on them," Joey said with a loopy grin. "But I didn't make any baby chicks . . . I only made a mess."

Yuck. The class laughed. Joey's cheeks turned red, but his smile quickly returned. He pulled out a piece of paper. It showed a

picture of a strange-looking chair. The middle part of the seat was cut out, making it look like the letter V. "I got this idea at Jigsaw's house," he said. "I was sitting at the corner of the table and I couldn't tuck my chair in all the way. I kept banging it on the table leg." He pointed to his drawing. "So I figured that if you cut out the middle part, the problem would be solved."

He gave a worried look to Ms. Gleason. "Is that all right?" he asked.

Ms. Gleason rose from her chair, beaming from earring to earring. Then, slowly, she began to clap. The rest of the class joined her. "Very nice job, Joey. Very good work!" she exclaimed. "I wouldn't mind having one of those chairs in my house."

Joey swallowed hard. "Really?"

"Really."

I laughed to myself. That Joey. It figured that his invention would be something that helped him get closer to the dinner table.

"Pssst, Jigsaw," Stringbean Noonan called from behind me. "Look what I got today."

He held up a piece of orange construction paper. It read: I SAW WHAT YOU DID.

I sighed. This case was getting on my nerves.

Chapter Fifteen

Goodness

That night, Mila called me. I told her about my adventures in the principal's office. She loved it. Then she changed the subject. "Three more notes came in school yesterday," Mila said. "Stringbean got one and so did Helen and Bobby."

I checked my journal. "That leaves only Danika, Joey, Eddie, and Geetha," I said.

"We have art class tomorrow," Mila said. "Let's keep an eye on everyone's supplies."

"Yes, like who owns a packet of multicolored construction paper," I said.

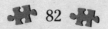 82

"Exactly."

In art with Mr. Manus, we were busy cutting out pictures from magazines for collages. Mila leaned toward me and said, "Three kids have multicolored construction paper — Bobby, Nicole, and Geetha."

Nicole had already received a blackmail note. But I couldn't rule her out as a suspect just yet. We'd have to check them all out, one by one. I walked over to Solofsky's desk. He cut away at his magazines like a lunatic. It was the sloppiest job I'd ever seen. "Hey, *Sports Illustrated for Kids*," I noted. I picked up one of his magazines and leafed through it. Plenty of pictures had been ripped out. But none of the letters.

I took a stroll over to Nicole's desk. She was struggling to get glue out of a tube. "Here, let me help," I offered. That gave me a chance to look over Nicole's shoulder. "Why aren't you doing a collage?" I wondered.

Nicole frowned. "I forgot my magazines," she confessed.

Suddenly, a shriek filled the room. "Hey, watch it with that glue, Jigsaw!"

I turned to see Mr. Manus frantically wiping his shoes. I must have squeezed the tube too hard. A stream of glue flew from the tube . . . through the air . . . onto his blue suede Hush Puppies.

After apologizing nine gazillion times to Mr. Manus, I turned my attention to Geetha Nair.

She was the last person I'd ever suspect of blackmail. But after I watched her closely, I knew it was true. Geetha was an artist. She used her scissors like a surgeon, cutting perfectly straight lines into the paper. No ragged cuts, no mistakes. Just like in the notes. Mila distracted her for me, while I "borrowed" a few of Geetha's magazines. There it was — the proof I needed. Many of the letters in the headlines had been carefully, perfectly cut out.

We confronted Geetha in the hallway outside room 201.

She shyly stared at the ground, hardly able to speak. "I don't understand, Geetha," Mila said. "Why have you been sending those awful notes?"

Geetha fidgeted for a moment, then lifted her eyes to me. "It was an experiment," she confessed.

"A what?"

"An experiment," she repeated, this time in a stronger voice. "I wanted to invent . . . *goodness.*"

"Goodness?" Mila echoed. "What do you mean?"

Again, Geetha nervously looked at the floor. "Sometimes kids can be mean," she said. "We all do bad things. And I just thought . . ."

She paused.

 86

"You thought . . . what?" I prodded.

"I thought that if we believed someone was watching us, then maybe we'd all treat one another nicer." She looked at Mila, then me. Her chocolate eyes looked like wet stones.

Mila spoke first. "That's a beautiful invention, Geetha."

"Maybe it wasn't the best way to go

about it," I pointed out. "But it's the thought that counts."

"Will you tell on me?" Geetha asked.

"No," Mila replied. "We won't tell. Besides, maybe your invention is working. Take a look for yourself."

We glanced around the hallway. Bobby Solofsky helped open a door for Ms. Gleason. Smiling politely, Kim let Nicole go ahead of her at the water fountain.

A shy grin flickered on Geetha's face. Her eyes lost that glassy look. Instead, they filled with hope.

"Let's go inside," I pointed out. "Eddie is supposed to show us his invention."

Chapter Sixteen
The Money Machine

First, Mila and Danika showed their invention. "We call them Krunch Berry Cookies," Danika said.

Mila held up a plate of cookies. Danika continued, "We did research on the lady who invented chocolate chip cookies. So we thought, why not invent a new cookie?!"

"We tried lots of different things," Mila added. "Bologna cookies . . . french fry cookies . . . all kinds of crazy stuff."

Danika added, "Then we decided on Krunch Berry Cookies!"

The boys in the class were making gross sounds, holding their stomachs and laughing at the same time.

Ms. Gleason gave us all a chance to try a cookie. I'll say this: They were crunchy. Disgusting. But definitely crunchy.

Then it was Eddie's turn. His invention was more than a little complicated.

"This is my automatic Monopoly Money Machine," Eddie said proudly. "It counts money. All you've got to do is take a marble and drop it down this shoot. It trips the spring, which pushes the lettuce, then the hungry hamster steps on the seesaw, forcing the glove to go down, and then . . ."

To tell you the truth, I could barely understand what he was talking about. I'll say this, it sure looked cool. Of course, it didn't work. The glove came down and threw Monopoly money all over the floor. If the idea was to make a mess, then it worked plenty good.

"It certainly is . . . er . . . *original*," Ms. Gleason concluded.

"*That's* a million-dollar idea?" I whispered to Mila. "It looks like a million-dollar waste of time."

Shhh. Mila placed a finger in front of her lips. "Uietqay," she said in pig Latin. "E'llhay earhay ouyay."

We laughed. And you know what? It felt good. After all, I'd had some week. A week

of weird inventions . . . creepy notes . . . and a visit to the principal's office. I looked around at the class. Everybody seemed happy, smiling, laughing together. Eddie had his invention back. He seemed happy, even if it didn't turn out to be a million-dollar idea. And there, sitting quietly at her desk, was Geetha.

Just watching.

Maybe we can invent goodness after all. I guess it's like a jigsaw puzzle. Or a mystery.

Just one piece at a time.

Puzzling Codes
and
Activities

How to Draw Jigsaw Jones

1

2

3

4

5

6

8

7

9

A good detective needs a good memory. Are you ready to test your brain power? Turn to pages 2 and 3. Now look at the picture for fifteen seconds. Ask a friend or family member to count from one to fifteen while you look. Then see if you can answer the questions below. But don't look back at the picture. That would be cheating!

1. How many people are sitting at the table?
2. Is Rags in the picture?
3. Is Jigsaw wearing his hat?
4. How many people are wearing glasses?
5. What food is Jigsaw holding up on his fork?

Answers on page 106.

Wacky Inventions Word Search

All inventions start with an idea. Here's an idea: Find the names of these inventions in the box below! Words can go across, up, or down.

Words: COOKIE, ZIPPER, FRISBEE, POPSICLE, BAND-AID

```
G T P Q Z V
C O O K I E
B X P G P E
A Z S Y P B
N G I D E S
D V C E R I
A U L C N R
I A E A S F
D M T O T E
```

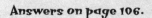

Answers on page 106.

Jigsaw Jones and Mila Yeh are an ace detective team. Sometimes they need to send top-secret messages to each another. Speaking in a secret language like pig Latin works well. But invisible notes are even better!

Invisible Ink

Jigsaw and Mila used invisible ink to solve *The Case of the Class Clown*. Here's how you can send top-secret messages using invisible ink:

1. First, dip a paintbrush in lemon juice. Then use the brush to write your message.
2. Next, pass the message to your partner.

To read the invisible note:

1. First, ask an adult to help mix a jar of water with a few drops of iodine.
2. Then, all your partner has to do is brush the water and iodine onto the paper. The message will magically appear!

TOP SECRET:
CHECK OUT CHAPTER TEN TO FIND OUT
HOW YOU CAN TALK IN CODE!

How to Draw Mila

1
4
7
2
5
8
3
6
9

How to Draw Rags

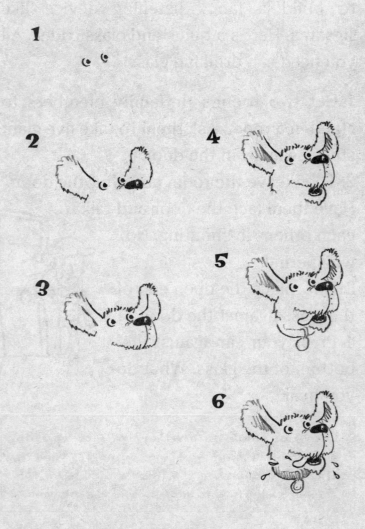

1

2

3

4

5

6

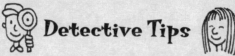

Detective Tips

Sometimes a detective doesn't have time to build a fancy listening device like Jigsaw's. Here's a quick and classic idea. All you need is a drinking glass!

1. Get two friends or family members to stand in a room. Ask them to take five giant steps away from the door.
2. Then leave the room and shut the door. Have them face the door and talk to each other. No shouting. No whispering.
3. Now place the open end of the glass against the door.
4. Press your ear against the bottom of the glass. What do you hear?

Can you think of another way to spy on someone without getting caught? Need a clue? Put together the jigsaw puzzle on the sticker sheet in this book to find the answer.

From the Top Secret Pages of Jigsaw Jones's Detective Journal

Now you can solve mysteries like Jigsaw Jones and Mila Yeh!

Case: The case of _____

Client: _____

Suspects: _____
_____

Clues: _____
_____

Key Words: _____
_____

Mystery Solved: _____
_____

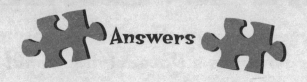

Answers

Million-Dollar Memory

1. Nine

2. Yes

3. No. It's on his chair.

4. Two. Joey and Grams.

5. Broccoli

Wacky Inventions Word Search

```
G T P Q Z V
C O O K I E
B X P G P E
A Z S Y P B
N G I D E S
D V C E R I
A U L C N R
I A E A S F
D M T O T E
```